The Mouse God

The Mouse God

By Richard Kennedy

Illustrated by Stephen Harvard

An Atlantic Monthly Press Book
Little, Brown and Company
BOSTON   TORONTO

FIRST EDITION

T 03/79

Library of Congress Cataloging in Publication Data

Kennedy, Richard.
    The mouse god.

    "An Atlantic Monthly Press book."
    SUMMARY: A vain and lazy barnyard cat makes a coat
of mouse skins to protect his fur while chasing mice.
The mice consider him their god and trust him to send
them to heaven.
    [1. Cats — Fiction. 2. Mice — Fiction] I. Harvard,
Stephen. II. Title.
PZ7.K385Mo   [E]   78-11731
ISBN 0-316-48904-2

ATLANTIC—LITTLE, BROWN BOOKS
ARE PUBLISHED BY
LITTLE, BROWN AND COMPANY
IN ASSOCIATION WITH
THE ATLANTIC MONTHLY PRESS

Published simultaneously in Canada
by Little, Brown & Company (Canada) Limited

PRINTED IN THE UNITED STATES OF AMERICA

For Vickie, the big sister.

Books by Richard Kennedy

The Parrot and the Thief
The Contests at Cowlick
The Porcelain Man
Oliver Hyde's Dishcloth Concert
Come Again in the Spring
The Blue Stone
The Rise and Fall of Ben Gizzard
The Dark Princess
The Mouse God

There was a large barnyard cat who was both vain and lazy, and he would have preferred of all things to lie upon a windowsill in the sun and love himself. But he had to earn his keep, so each day he attended to chasing mice and sent a good number of them off to eternity.

The constant hunting was a terror to the mice, but also a grief to the cat, for he mussed and dirtied his fine coat as he chased his quarry under the floorboards, across the roof beams, and through all manner of grimy and dusty places. He had a small mirror to look into, and it distressed him awfully to come back to the shed he lived in and find his fur so tangled and dirty. It sometimes took him half a day after a chase to put his fur in order again, and he would sit on his windowsill licking at himself and hating the mice, for he blamed them that he did not have enough leisure time to himself.

And then one night he awoke in the middle of a dream. "Why, yes!" he said. He had the solution. "I will only need some coveralls such as the farmer wears, and that way I shall remain practically clean no matter where I must chase

the mice." He went to sleep again, and in the morning over his bowl of milk he concluded his plans. He would begin saving mouse skins to make himself a sleek coat that he could move about in as quickly and smoothly as in his own coat of fur. This way he would keep his own fur clean. Once a week he could wash out the mouse coat in the creek and save several hours of his own time each day. He could spend this time napping and admiring himself in his mirror.

And so it was that the cat began catching the mice by their heads so to save their skins in one piece, and he got salt and alum to cure the tiny pelts, and he pinned them to the wall of the shed to dry. In a month's time he had enough pelts to make himself a coat. He took needle and thread then, and sitting cross-legged in the corner of the shed, he began working on the garment.

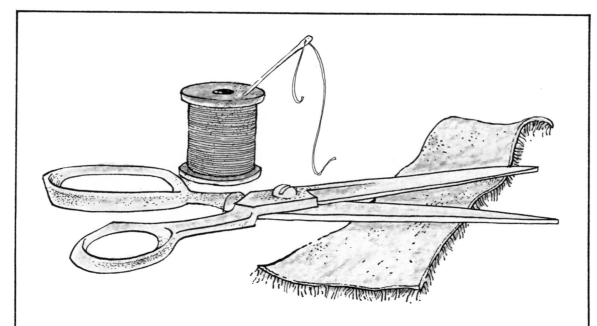

"Pockets inside or out?" he wondered as he worked and planned on the coat. "Inside, to be sure, so they won't snag on anything in the chase." He worked on, sewing the pelts together. "Shall it have a belt?" He thought on this for a while. "Yes, a belt to tighten the coat when I scramble through small places, that is a good idea." He sewed on. "A collar? Yes, a collar of course, to snug up close around my ears in cold weather. And shall I

make it with a zipper down the front, or with
buttons? Hmmmmmmm. Buttons will do."
And he continued sewing on his mouse-skin
coat, and presently had it all finished.

He put it on and stood in front of his mirror.
It fit beautifully. "Stylish," said the cat, turning
this way and that. He found that he had enough
mouse skins left over for a pair of boots, so he
finished those and looked at himself again.
"Dainty," he said, pointing his toes. Still there
was more fur left, so he made himself a hat.
He made it with a brim, and also earflaps.
"It will keep the cobwebs out of my ears,"
said the cat, and he looked at himself again.
"Smart!" he said, and he picked up a sparrow
feather and stuck it in the hat. He looked again,
and winked at himself. "Why, the hat should
set a fashion all by itself," he said. Then he
went out on the hunt.

The coat and boots and hat hardly hindered him at all, and he came upon a mouse around a corner of the barn and set himself to spring at the creature as soon as it should recover from its fright. But the mouse only lay there on the ground, staring with its little eyes wide open.

The cat was quite a sight. He stood perfectly
still also, for those are the rules of a cat-and-
mouse chase. The mouse must run first. But the
mouse did not run. When it had quite gotten
over its awe, it called out, "Friends, cousins,
brothers, sisters! Come out, come out!
The mouse god has come to visit us!"

Well! And yet you know, it might be imagined—a large cat covered all over with mouse skins just might be mistaken for a mouse god. The cat understood this at once, and waited perfectly still to see what else should come of the matter. Then other mice appeared, and in great wonder at the sight of the cat in his mouse coat, they lay down all around him in reverence until at last the cat was surrounded by dozens of mice, all of them waiting for the great mouse god to break his silence.

Now, the cat saw that he had come upon a wonderful opportunity if only he could use it right. It would not do to run among the mice. He might catch a half-dozen of them, but if he played his role of the mouse god cleverly, he might get them all at a single catch. Therefore, he thought carefully and came up with his plan. He addressed the mice thus:

"Children, I have been watching you from heaven, and although you are good mice, you could be better. And so I have come to set you on the path that will surely lead you to heaven. Do you wish to go to heaven?"

"Oh, yes," cried the mice, "we all wish to go to heaven."

"Good," said the cat. "Then you must go to church, and you must praise me and sing hymns."

"But we have no church," the mice said.

"Then you must build one," said the cat. "Over there is a large crate. That will do quite nicely. Clean it out, make a wide door, put benches in it, and paint it white. And when I come around on next Sunday morning, I expect to find all of you inside singing hymns."

"Shall we make a steeple for it?"

"Naturally," said the cat.

"And colored glass for the windows?"

"Exactly," said the cat. "And you shall all
be well on your way to heaven by next Sunday.
Now go home and meditate on the job before
you, and I will go back to heaven."

The mice ran off, and the cat crept back to
his shed. Later in the day the mice got busy
making the old crate into a church, and the
cat watched out of his window.

The mice worked that day and all the next,
which was Saturday, and the cat lay lazily on
his sill and watched them. The church was
coming along nicely. Near the end of the day

the mice moved the benches in, and then they painted the crate white. The cat went to his supply chest and got out a length of rope and tested its strength by tugging at a doorknob. "This should do," he said.

The next morning it was Sunday, and the cat watched while all the mice filed solemnly into their fine and bright new church. The steeple pointed to heaven and the colored windows sparkled in the sun. The cat put on his coat and boots and hat, and when he heard the mice singing hymns, he took his piece of rope and went out to the church. He listened for a while to the mice singing for their salvation, and he smiled. His plan was to throw the rope around the crate and drag it to the bridge over the river and dump it in, thus to be done with the mice forever. He knocked on the roof of the crate. "That's very

nice singing, my children, and it makes me happy to know you are all in church."

"Is that you, God?" they cried.

"Oh, yes," said the cat, throwing the rope around the crate and tightening it over the doors. Then he took the rope over his shoulder and began dragging the crate toward the bridge.

"Where are you taking us, God?" the mice cried out.

"To heaven, my children, straight to heaven. Sing bravely, now."

And the mice continued to sing as the cat lurched forward on his rope and dragged the crate up the road toward the bridge. At last he had the crate on the bridge. He looped the rope twice more around the crate and knotted it over the doors. Then he prepared to lift it over the rail and dump it in the river. The mice sang:

We all love you, if you please,
give to us our daily cheese.

The cat struggled with the crate but could not find a good grip on it. Besides that, it was too heavy for him to lift. He set the corner down and wondered what to do. The mice sang:

We all sing and praise you that
you will save us from the cat.

Along came a closed wagon, and it rumbled up onto the bridge. On the side of the wagon

25

were written in colorful paints such things as
these:

> ISAIAH 12:5
> LUKE 12:32
> MATTHEW 19:14
> LUKE 17:21
> 23RD PSALM

For these are references to the Bible, and this
was the wagon of an old traveling preacher.
When the wagon was opposite the crate and
the cat, the old man pulled up his horse and
listened to the mice singing hymns in their
pretty soprano voices.

"Young man," said the preacher to the cat
(he did not see too well), "that is the most
astounding music box I have ever heard. And
how clever, to have it made to look just like a
small church. I would give a good amount to

have such a thing for myself, for I am not able
to offer the faithful any music of my own."

The mice began another hymn.

The cat considered. "Do you travel far?"
he asked the preacher.

"Clear across the country," said the old man.
"From one end of the land to the other, spread-
ing the good word and teaching righteousness."

The cat thought on this. If he gave the crate
to the old preacher, the mice would be gone
forever. That would be as good as drowning
them.

"The box is yours," said the cat. "Remember
me in your prayers."

The preacher loaded the crate into the back
of his wagon and started on his way again.
He waved to the cat, and called out, "Thanks
be to God."

"You're welcome," said the cat.

And that is the end of the story for the cat. He went back to his shed and lay down on the windowsill in the sun.

As for the mice, they stopped singing after a while and cried out, "Are we in heaven yet?" The preacher went around to the back of his wagon and threw off the rope from the crate and opened the doors. He was quite surprised that it was not a music box, but a box filled with singing mice, yet he was not at all disappointed. He took care not to frighten the small creatures, and fed them some cheese. In the next few days he built them little tables and chairs and beds, and gave them a whole half of his wagon to live in. He let them run in the fields and kept them safe and set out as good meals for them as he did for himself, and they lived happily together.

When the people gathered around the wagon

to hear the old man preach, the mice went into the crate and sang hymns, so many people were fortunate to hear their sweet voices. Now and then they would ask the old preacher if they were in heaven yet.

"Are you not happy?" asked the old man.

"Very happy," said the mice.

"Then you are in heaven," said the preacher. "Sing 'amen,' children."

"*Aaaaaaa . . . men*," sang the mice.

Amen.